Hoke

D1418541

"Before I formed you in your
mother's body I chose you.
Before you were born
I set you apart to serve me."
—*Jeremiah 1:5 NIrV*

I Am a Promise
ISBN-10: 0-310-70075-2
ISBN-13: 978-0-310-70075-3
Copyright © 2002 by Gloria Gaither
Illustrations copyright © 2002 by Kristina Stephenson

Requests for information should be addressed to:
Grand Rapids, Michigan 49530

Editor: Barbara J. Scott
Interior Design: Lisa Workman
Art Direction: Laura Maitner

Printed in China

07 08 09 10 • 11 10 9 8

I Am a Promise

Written by *Gloria Gaither*
Illustrated by *Kristina Stephenson*

ZONDERkidz

ZONDERVAN.com/
AUTHORTRACKER
follow your favorite authors

"Wow, you've been everywhere, Grandpa!" Jeffrey said.

"Yeah!" his friends agreed.

"Someday," Grandpa said, "if God wants you to, you'll go to faraway places too. All of you will grow up to be everything God wants you to be."

"Really? You mean . . ."

"I can go anywhere
that he wants me to go?"

"You can go anywhere
that he wants you to go."

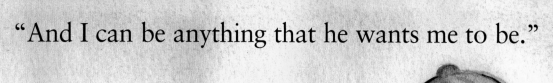

"And I can be anything that he wants me to be."

"You can be anything—
anything God wants you to be."

"I can know anything
that he wants me to know."

"You can know anything
God wants you to know."

"I can say anything that he wants me to say."

"Well, I can climb
the high mountain."

"I can cross the wide sea."

"I'm a
great big promise you see."

"I am a promise. I am a possibility."

"I am a promise, with a capital P."

"I am a great big bundle
of potentiality."

"And I am learnin' to hear God's voice."

"And I am tryin'
to make the right choices."

"I'm a promise to be . . .

anything God wants me to be."

"She's a promise to be . . .

anything God
wants her to be."

anything God
wants me to be."

Now *you* say it...

"I am a promise to be..."

anything God wants me to be."

"With every baby born, children,
God makes a promise to the world.
You are no exception!
No matter who you are or where you live,
your life holds wonderful promises
to bless the family of God
in a way that only you can!
You are special!"

"Even me?"

"You bet! God loves you
very, very much.
Why, you're a promise
with a capital P!"

"I know the plans I have for you," announces the LORD.
"I want you to enjoy success. I do not plan to harm you.
I will give you hope for the years to come."
—*Jeremiah 29:11 NIrV*